THE ELEPHANT
from BAGHDAD

by Mary Tavener Holmes & John Harris

illustrated by Jon Cannell

MARSHALL CAVENDISH CHILDREN

Marshall Cavendish Corporation, 99 White Plains Road, Tarrytown, NY 10591
www.marshallcavendish.us/kids

Ivory chess pieces on title page, Bibliothèque Nationale, Paris. Photo: Erich Lessing/Art Resource, NY; Bust of Emperor Charlemagne, Cathedral Treasury, Palatine Chapel, Aachen, Germany. Photo: Erich Lessing/Art Resource, NY; Portrait of Harun al-Rashid, hero of the Arabian Nights, Indian miniature, signed Behzad, Bibliothèque Nationale, Paris. Photo: Snark/Art Resource, NY; Water jug, cloisonné enamel, Treasury of the Abbey of Saint-Maurice, Valais, Switzerland. Photo: Giraudon/The Bridgeman Art Library; Saber and scabbard, Säbel Karls d. Grossen. Photo: Kunsthistorisches Museum, Vienna; Silk Cloth with Elephants in Medallions, Cathedral Treasure, Palatine Chapel, Aachen, Germany. Photo: Scala/Art Resource, NY.

Library of Congress Cataloging-in-Publication Data
Holmes, Mary Tavener.
The elephant from Baghdad / by Mary Tavener Holmes and John Harris ;
illustrated by Jon Cannell. — 1st ed.
    p. cm.
Includes bibliographical references.
Summary: Relates the story, told by a monk named Notker the Stammerer, of how the Emperor Charlemagne sent an ambassador to Baghdad, the center of theMuslim world, to learn about the great ruler in the East, Haroun al Rashid. Includes notes on the factual basis of the story.
ISBN 978-0-7614-6111-1 (hardcover) — ISBN 978-0-7614-6112-8 (ebook)
1. Charlemagne, Emperor, 742-814—Juvenile fiction. 2. Harun al-Rashid, Caliph, ca. 763-809—Juvenile fiction. [1. Charlemagne, Emperor, 742-814—Fiction. 2. Harun al-Rashid, Caliph, ca. 763-809—Fiction. 3. Elephants—Fiction. 4. Islamic Empire—History—750-1258—Fiction.] I. Harris, John, 1950 July 7- II. Cannell, Jon, ill. III. Title.
PZ7.H7373El 2012
    [E]—dc23
    2011016401

The illustrations are rendered in watercolor and ink.
Book design by Jon Cannell
Editor: Margery Cuyler
Printed in China (E)
First edition
1 3 5 6 4 2

 Marshall Cavendish
Children

To the Geren Gang
—M.T.H

For John & Ed
—J.H.

For Kjerstin, Torsten,
Solvej & Jensen
—J.C.

THE GREAT MAN, more than six feet tall, would stride to the edge of the hot springs, throw off his robe, and slide into the bubbling water. The elephant, so pale that he all but disappeared in the steam, would wade in slowly next to him. Then the two friends would paddle about contentedly side by side.

Who were these two amazing creatures?

ABU

CHARLEMAGNE

One was Abu the elephant, who had come all the way from Baghdad, the center of the Muslim world. The other was Charlemagne, who ruled over most of Europe from his striped and stony palace in the ancient city of Aachen, Germany. How did this come to pass?

Let me explain as best I can, although I am but a humble monk, Notker the Stammerer, asked to set down this story by my abbot. And yes, I stammer. But not when I sing.

Tall, broad shouldered, and immensely strong, Charlemagne had blond hair and a mustache that stretched from ear to ear. He carried a huge golden sword to show his power and strength.

This golden bust of Charlemagne holds a piece of the emperor's skull.

Joyeuse, the sword used to crown the kings of France.

CHARLEMAGNE
(742–814 CE)

HARUN AL-RASHID
(763–809 CE)

Charlemagne was a very curious man. He had heard stories about a great ruler in the East and decided he must learn more about him. That man was the legendary Harun al–Rashid, caliph of Baghdad.

So Charlemagne sent some trusted men of his court to meet the great Harun. They traveled thousands of miles, from Germany, across the Alps to Italy, and finally by boat across the Mediterranean.

BAGHDAD

• CAIRO

When the Europeans arrived in Baghdad, they were amazed by what they saw. There were singers in the streets, scholars arguing, hundreds of beautiful buildings and libraries and mosques, minarets reaching up to the sky, and brilliant tiles shining on the walls.

In the center of this great city, Harun lived in a fantastic golden palace. He welcomed the ambassadors with open arms.

Like Charlemagne, Harun was curious. He wanted to learn all about the powerful man in the West.

For weeks, then months, Harun introduced Charlemagne's men to artists, musicians, scholars, mathematicians, architects, and poets. The ambassadors were astounded by what they saw and learned. The people in Baghdad seemed to know things the Europeans did not — about science, medicine, engineering, and art. The Europeans were treated to concerts and fine meals, even sherbet made of snow.

All these marvels are true. I swear it.

At last it came time for the ambassadors to return to Charlemagne's court. But Harun al-Rashid did not want them to go back empty handed. He loaded a caravan with presents fit for a fellow emperor.

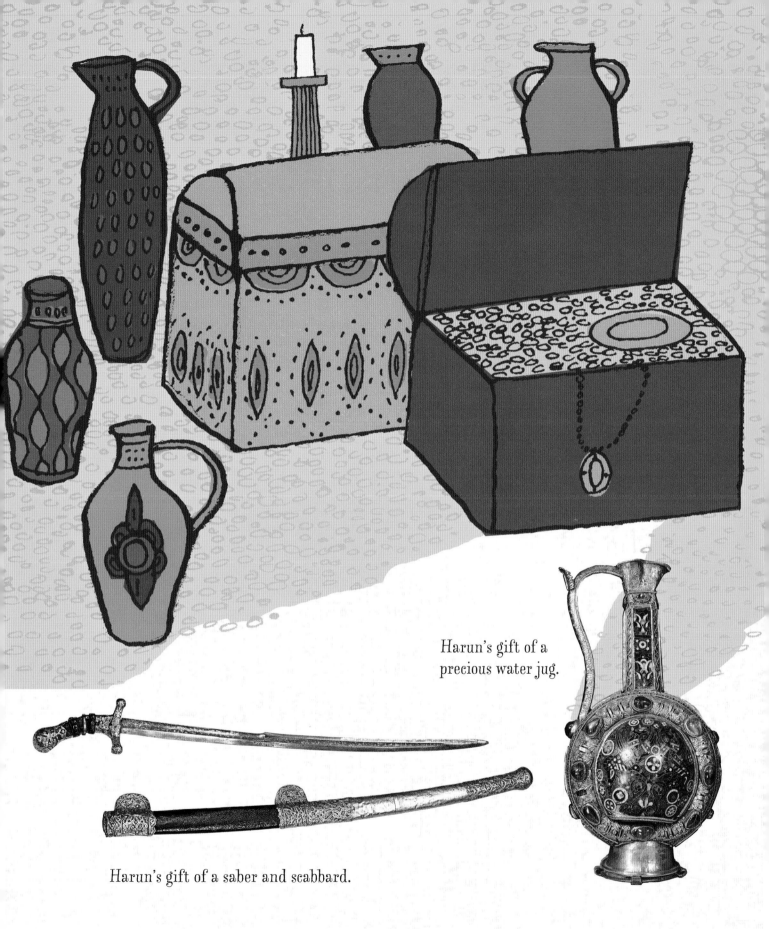

Harun's gift of a
precious water jug.

Harun's gift of a saber and scabbard.

But these gifts were not enough.

And so Harun ordered his artisans to create a magnificent clock. At each hour, brass weights would drop on a cymbal to announce the time. On the clock's face were twelve doors. As the bell sounded, a door would open and out would ride a mechanical horseman.

This clock was like something out of the magical stories known as the Arabian Nights.

But even this new treasure was not enough.

Harun wanted to send one MORE precious present to the great emperor of the West.

He thought and thought and finally decided that the only present worthy of Charlemagne was the rarest of rare treasures in his court: the elephant named Abu.

Abu was born with no color in his skin, which caused him to be white.
He was so valuable that he had his own keeper, a Jewish man named Isaac.
Isaac went where Abu went, ate where Abu ate, and slept where Abu slept.
So, of course, Isaac would have to join Charlemagne's ambassadors
as they started on their long journey home.

With the clock and other treasures, the party set out from Baghdad.
Sitting on a platform on top of Abu was Harun's magnificent clock:
a gift on top of a gift for the emperor Charlemagne.

What an astonishing sight they must have made, this caravan.
But it is true. I swear it.

They followed the same route taken by the famous general Hannibal when he crossed the Alps with thirty-seven elephants five hundred years before.

What a journey! The towering peaks covered with snow, the road that wound its way through steep mountains and dropped a thousand feet, so narrow that they could see over the edge. . . .

Finally, in July of the year 802, after being gone for almost two years, the caravan arrived back at the court of Charlemagne.

I do not know which delighted Charlemagne more: the immense and complicated clock or Abu. The elephant raised his trunk in the air as Isaac paraded him through the cobbled streets. It was as if Abu were saying to the cheering crowds, "I salute you!"

Charlemagne invited Abu and Isaac to live in his palace. Once or twice a day, Charlemagne would visit his immense guest as he ate the mounds of grass and bark that were brought to him each morning.

An enormous cistern always was kept full of fresh water, and Charlemagne would watch Abu as he dipped his trunk, sucked up water, and squirted it into his mouth— or over his body. What a shower!

Charlemagne showed off the beautiful Abu to visiting princes and kings. The emperor's many children came to stare at Abu. Charlemagne ordered the artists of his court to create portraits of the extraordinary creature. Abu's image began to appear on coins and tapestries throughout the empire.

Silk cloth woven with elephants found in Charlemagne's tomb in the city of Aachen (known today as Aix-la-Chapelle).

Charlemagne even dressed Abu in armor and led him into battle against his Danish enemies. The soldiers were so frightened when they saw the white elephant, they dropped their weapons and fled. They thought Abu had been summoned up by magic!

Abu, like his master, began to grow old. Charlemagne had a house built just for him and Isaac near a river in the town of Augsburg, where Abu could take his daily bath. Charlemagne sometimes visited his friend and patted his trunk. "Hello, my brave one," he would say.

Finally, in the year 810, Abu died.

When Charlemagne learned of the death of his old friend, he wept.

Who would have thought that the emperor of the West would find such companionship with a white elephant from the East?

Yet I think I see why. Each of them was unusual—and by some strange circumstance, they understood each other. A man and an elephant, you say? How could that be possible?

But it was. I swear it. It was.

A NOTE FROM THE AUTHORS

NOTKER THE STAMMERER (840-912 CE)

We have imagined the narrator of our story to be Notker the Stammerer, monk of St. Gall, who did, in fact, speak with a stammer. He was the historian for the abbey of St. Gall in the Swiss Alps, a monastery founded by Charlemagne's father, Pepin the Short. Notker wrote his chronicle of Charlemagne's life between the years 883 and 884. Our other main source of information about Charlemagne was the chronicle begun around 826 by Einhard (770-840 CE), a courtier and secretary to Charlemagne himself.

THE MAGICAL MECHANICAL WATER CLOCK

In the ninth century the Arabs were famous for their elaborate mechanical devices and timepieces. Harun al-Rashid's gift to Charlemagne disappeared long ago, but it was described in detail in the 807 CE *Annales regni Francorum*, a journal that chronicled the daily life in Charlemagne's court:

"A marvelous mechanical contraption, in which the course of the twelve hours moved according to a water clock, with as many brazen little balls, which fell down on the hour and through their fall made a cymbal ring underneath. On this clock there were also twelve horsemen who at the end of each hour stepped out of twelve windows, closing the previously open windows by their movements."
The illustrator, Jon Cannell, based his illustrations of the clock on the description above and on another clock design that was drawn in 1205-1206 (four hundred years after Harun) by Al-Jazazi in his *Book of Knowledge of Ingenious Mechanical Devices*, which is in the Library of the Topkapi Sarayi Muzesi in Istanbul, Turkey.

The main sources for our story are *Einhard and Notker the Stammerer: Two Lives of Charlemagne*, translated by David Ganz (Penguin Books, 2008), and the catalog of the exhibition *Ex Oriente: Geschichte und Gegenwart Christlicher, Jüdischer und Islamisher Kulturen* (Aachen, 2003).